Slaughtered Nursery Rhymes
For Grown-Ups

Written by Ian Hooper

Illustrations by Mike Porter

Illustrations by: Mike Porter | mikeporterart@yahoo.com

For our Inner Child
and its hidden demons

Little Jack Horner

Little Jack Horner sat in the corner,
eating his cannibal pie,
he put in his thumb and pulled out a tongue,
then a nose and a cheek and an eye.

The making of it had taken some time,
but Jack was patient and neat.
He'd waited all day for the thug of a boy
who lived at the end of the street.

A crash of his skull and a drag on his neck,
and before you'd have known, twas done.
Then cut him up fine, add a good pastry lid,
with a glaze that shines like the sun.

For little Jack Horner who sits in the corner,
is a killer that's best left alone.
Don't shout out rude names, nor tease, nor cajole
when you're making your own way back home.

Just be quite polite, maybe say *how'd you do?*
Or give him a wave passing by
for if you are rude, he'll serve cold revenge
And you'll be the meat in his pie...

Little Miss Muffet

Little Miss Muffet sat on a tuffet,
poking the knife into Kay
when along came a copper
who tried hard to stop her
And Miss Muffet was taken away

Now the poor little miss, gives her mother a kiss,
as she's led up the steps to the rope,
and her rhyme won't be sung,
when Miss Muffet is hung,
and her mother is left without hope.

Little Bo Peep

Little Bo Peep has got no feet
nor legs all the way to her knees
For she fell fast asleep in a common so sweet,
with flowers and the buzzing of bees

But she slept for too long and was soon in a throng
of carnivorous sheep milling round
they sprang their attack and Bo Peep was too slack
to get up from her bed on the ground

The Sheep (and their Lambs) had considered their plans
and they knew that Bo Peep could not brook
A woolly onslaught, in the manner they fought
But they had to watch out for her crook

So for them to be winners, and have Bo Peep dinners
The sheep called for help, 'cos they could
Disguised in a fleece, Mister wolf wouldn't cease
Till he'd munched up that crook made of wood

Then he sauntered away, left the sheep to their play
And pondered poor Bo's awful plight
As he lay himself down, in his fleecy nightgown
Counting Sheep, killing Peep, in the night...

Old King Cole

Old King Cole was a merry old soul
And a merry old soul was he;
For his liver was shot, and abstain he could not
From the finest of wine and whiskey

And when he would ask for another small glass
His servants would rush here and there
And if not fast enough then their treatment was rough
For the old sozzled King wasn't fair

And the darling old Queen thought he was quite mean
always calling for this and for that
She'd had quite enough and was in quite the huff
As she lifted an old cricket bat

And when her dear hubby, all red fat and chubby
demanded a pipe and a bowl
she lifted the bat and with one mighty crack
brought an end to the reign of old Cole

Now she spends every day, making merry in play
and her subjects all queue up to see
Old widowed Queen Cole, the new diva of soul
And her band, The Fiddlers Three.

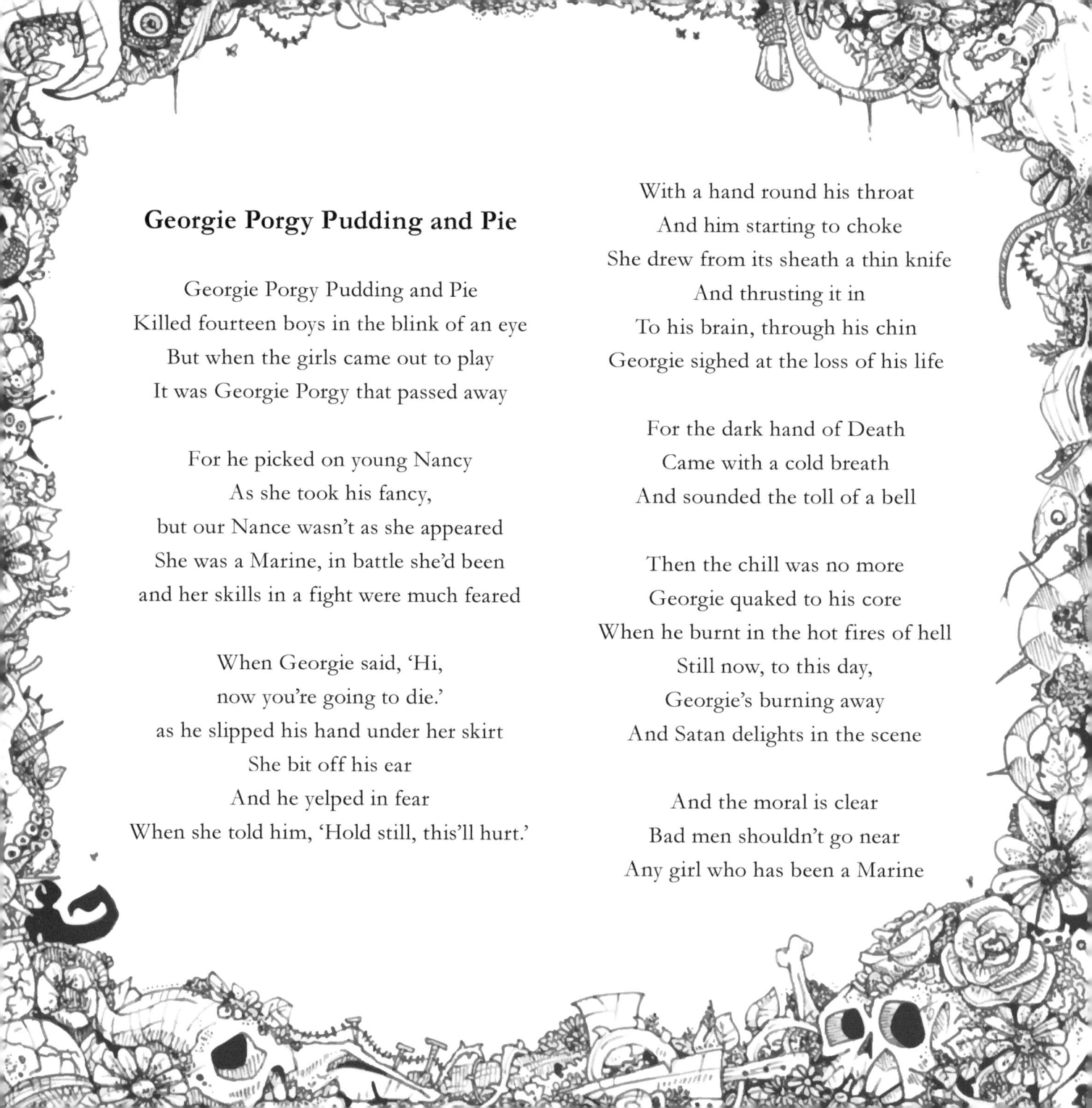

Georgie Porgy Pudding and Pie

Georgie Porgy Pudding and Pie
Killed fourteen boys in the blink of an eye
But when the girls came out to play
It was Georgie Porgy that passed away

For he picked on young Nancy
As she took his fancy,
but our Nance wasn't as she appeared
She was a Marine, in battle she'd been
and her skills in a fight were much feared

When Georgie said, 'Hi,
now you're going to die.'
as he slipped his hand under her skirt
She bit off his ear
And he yelped in fear
When she told him, 'Hold still, this'll hurt.'

With a hand round his throat
And him starting to choke
She drew from its sheath a thin knife
And thrusting it in
To his brain, through his chin
Georgie sighed at the loss of his life

For the dark hand of Death
Came with a cold breath
And sounded the toll of a bell

Then the chill was no more
Georgie quaked to his core
When he burnt in the hot fires of hell
Still now, to this day,
Georgie's burning away
And Satan delights in the scene

And the moral is clear
Bad men shouldn't go near
Any girl who has been a Marine

Hey Diddle Diddle

Hey Diddle Diddle, it's easy to fiddle
your tax returns
when they're online

The problems arise
when the auditor spies
a glaring and obvious sign

For your income is low
and so she will know
you can't buy four cars and a yacht

They'll impound all your stuff
And you'll have to live rough
For if you return you'll be caught

So you start out again
With a new life, in Spain
And there you are happy and free

For you had a stash
Of a million in cash

That the auditor just didn't see.
And in her report
To the judge in the court
The auditor sighed and was sad
You had gotten away
For your crime you'd not pay
And for that she felt terribly bad

She resigned the next day
A career thrown away
But what's this, she now lives in Spain?

For your million in cash
Was only half of your stash
And to share it was not such a pain

A bribe of that sum
Was a better outcome
Than the jail where they'd put you away

So now you both meet
On a hot Spanish street
And drink to how crime doesn't pay.

Jack and Jill

Jack and Jill went up the hill
and down into the valley
Jack knew that he would take her soon
Another for his tally

Her golden hair, her looks so fair
She'd enticed him with her tricks
So he'd do to her, what he'd done before
For a killer needs his fix

She laughed and skipped, then almost tripped
Letting out a tender cry
Jack pushed her down upon the ground
And shoved her skirt up high.

He'd have his fun, in the summer sun
Then he'd maximise the thrill
As he sliced her into little bits
Taking pleasure in the kill

He held her down, but then a frown
As she threw him to one side
And from her purse she drew a gun
Jack flinched and stared wide-eyed

You think I'm Jill from down the hill
But you're mistaken, mister,

My name is Tilly Dooleen
And young Clara was my sister

In his mind's eye he saw Clara die
By the slashing of his knife
She'd been his tenth and he'd enjoyed it most
When she'd begged him for her life

'Ah! Your sister was a treasure
And I did enjoy the pleasure,
But you have no proof, to get me put away
So put down your gun and do it quick, before I spoil your day

For you won't kill, my dearest Till'
You can't commit a crime
But I take delight in ending life
And you're on borrowed time.'

Jack knew no fear
His mind was clear
But he'd made a mighty blunder
For Tilly calmly raised her gun
And blew his brains asunder.

No Jack, nor Jill
Went up the hill
But Tilly made the climb
And in memory of poor Clara
She has penned this little rhyme.

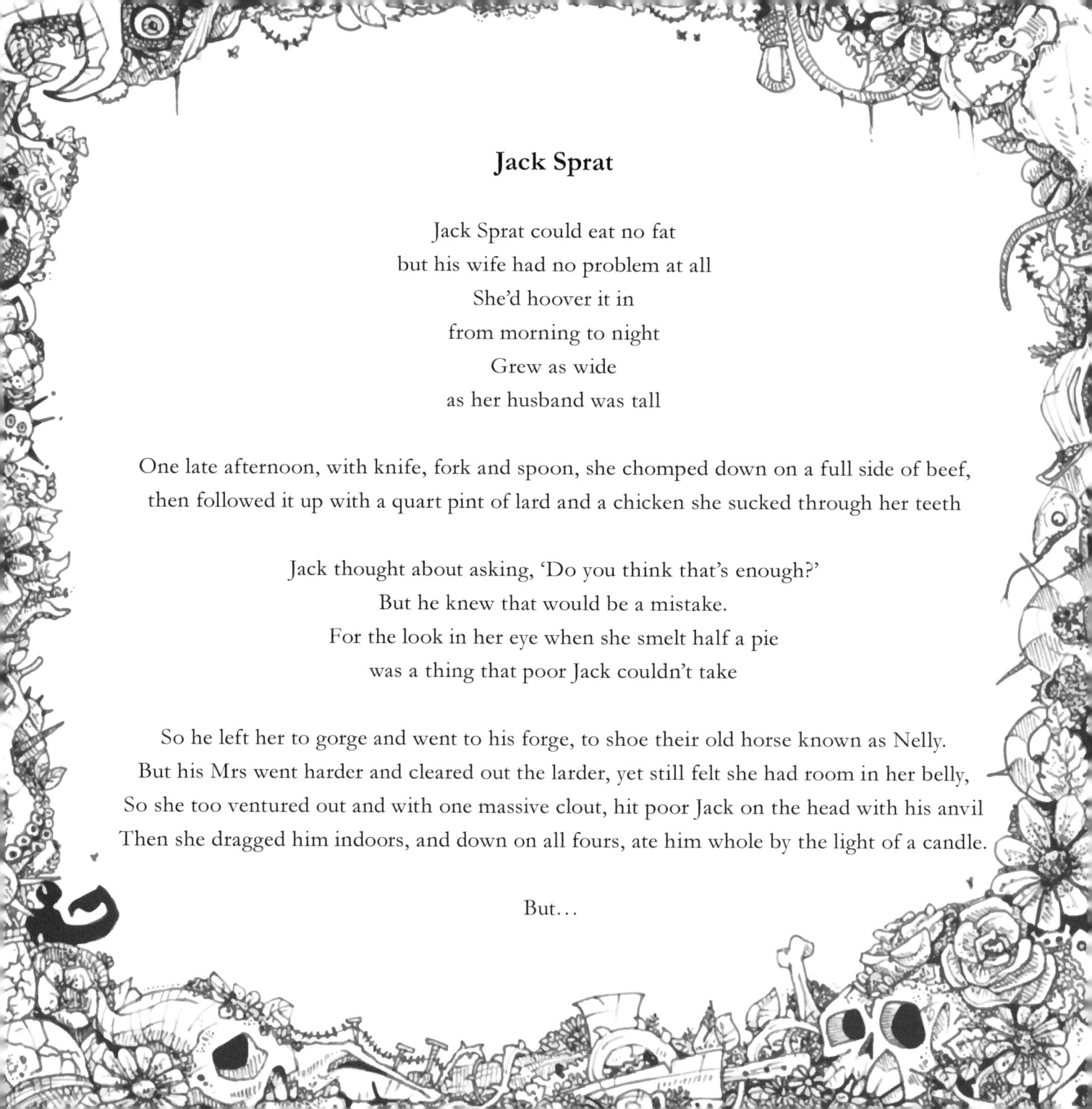

Jack Sprat

Jack Sprat could eat no fat
but his wife had no problem at all
She'd hoover it in
from morning to night
Grew as wide
as her husband was tall

One late afternoon, with knife, fork and spoon, she chomped down on a full side of beef,
then followed it up with a quart pint of lard and a chicken she sucked through her teeth

Jack thought about asking, 'Do you think that's enough?'
But he knew that would be a mistake.
For the look in her eye when she smelt half a pie
was a thing that poor Jack couldn't take

So he left her to gorge and went to his forge, to shoe their old horse known as Nelly.
But his Mrs went harder and cleared out the larder, yet still felt she had room in her belly,
So she too ventured out and with one massive clout, hit poor Jack on the head with his anvil
Then she dragged him indoors, and down on all fours, ate him whole by the light of a candle.

But…

The last laugh was Jack's, for he was still slim
And his Mrs could stomach no lean
She choked on his spine and died at half nine
Whilst Nelly looked on at the scene

Then Jack's head appeared, and at Nelly he leered
The horse almost shied right away
But with a toss of her mane, she stayed all the same
And approvingly, gave a low neigh

Jack fought his way free by elbow and knee
And fell to the floor with a clatter
And though he was bruised, he was quite amused
that his Mrs had grown no fatter

He looked down at her corpse and with no remorse
he told her she'd had quite the nerve
To ignore his devotion when she'd taken the notion
to see him as just an hors d'oeuvre
Then he stoked the forge fire, and made it a pyre
For the large and rotund Mrs Sprat

And the bellows did blow,
and the fire it did glow,
burning hot with a half-ton of fat.

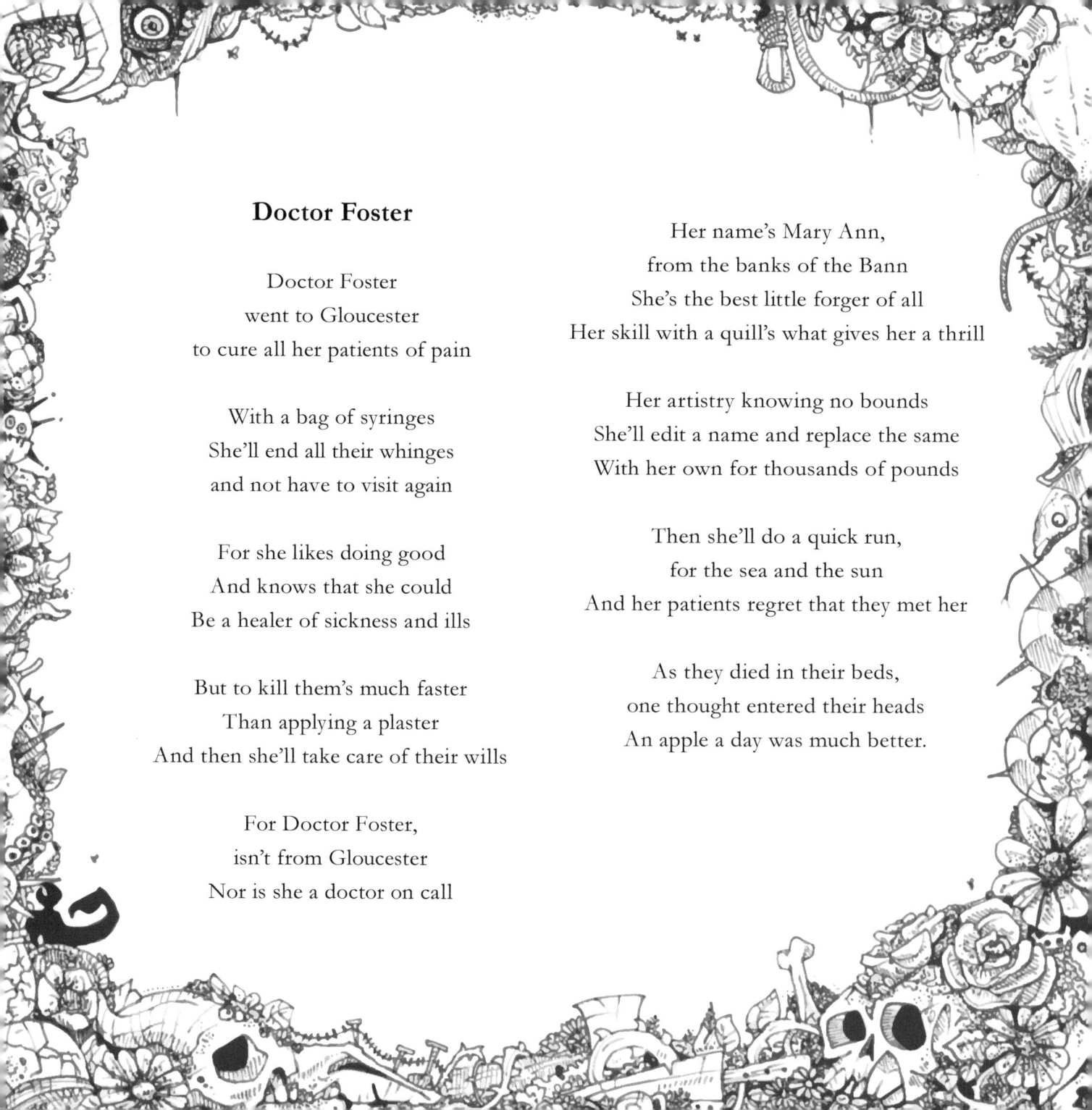

Doctor Foster

Doctor Foster
went to Gloucester
to cure all her patients of pain

With a bag of syringes
She'll end all their whinges
and not have to visit again

For she likes doing good
And knows that she could
Be a healer of sickness and ills

But to kill them's much faster
Than applying a plaster
And then she'll take care of their wills

For Doctor Foster,
isn't from Gloucester
Nor is she a doctor on call

Her name's Mary Ann,
from the banks of the Bann
She's the best little forger of all
Her skill with a quill's what gives her a thrill

Her artistry knowing no bounds
She'll edit a name and replace the same
With her own for thousands of pounds

Then she'll do a quick run,
for the sea and the sun
And her patients regret that they met her

As they died in their beds,
one thought entered their heads
An apple a day was much better.

It's Raining, It's Pouring

It's raining, it's pouring, my old man is snoring
When he's in bed, I'll bash in his head
And he won't get up in the morning

Jack be Nimble

Jack be nimble, Jack be quick
Pass me over the candlestick

Now come with me
to the ballroom dear
There's something that
you'll want to hear

I know that you have been untrue
I don't expect much else of you
And so my darling let this sink in
I know all about your little fling

And now I swing this candlestick
To bring it down on a head so thick
You had no clue I'd upped the money
To be paid out, on your death, honey

All that's left is to mask the deed
So the police will never need
To investigate this as a crime
As I don't fancy doing time

I shan't fret too much nor hide away
For no detectives worth their pay
Will miss the clues I leave around
To make them think you fell to ground

From the ladder that you used
To change a lightbulb that had fused
And no detective could be so thick
As to believe a candlestick

In the ballroom, laid you low
For that's not how real murders go
So I shan't fear the copper's knock
I'm the grieving widow of Jack Peacock.

Mary, Mary, quite contrary,

Mary, Mary, quite contrary,
What's in your garden that grows?

'That's coca, that's poppy, some cannabis too
Not forgetting the mushrooms, just here.
All watered and tended, by little old me,
Pray tell, why you're asking, my dear?'

I just want to be certain, I get all the plants
Their names and their species just so,
For the Judge and the Jury will need all the facts
when you appear down at the Bow

'Oh! Am I going to go on a trip?
That's nice, for I rarely get out.'

Yes a trip is quite fitting for what you'll be on
And I think you'll be gone, round about
A straight seven years perhaps a few less
Depends if the Judge feels benign.

'Oh don't be silly, he won't lock me up.
That Judge is a nephew of mine.
When he was little I taught him to grow
his own plants for personal use.
He'll hear the case and he'll fine me I'm sure,
but then he will let me go loose.
I'll not spend a day in old Holloway,
I'm too well connected for that.
The great and the good will want to ensure
I keep their names under my hat

Aww, don't look too glum,
you were not to know
when you eagerly slapped me in cuffs
Come here, have a seat,
take the weight of your feet
relax and take a few puffs
For my name is Mary and yes I'm contrary,
But gosh how my garden does grow

There's poppy and coca and mushrooms as well
and cannabis all in a row.'

Mary Has A Little Lamb

Mary has a little lamb
she loves the way it hops
she takes it to the shed today
to make it into chops.

Acknowledgements

As with all my books there was not a chance of this one seeing the light of day without an enormous amount of support and help being offered to me. Principally of course, for an illustrated book, my thanks must go to the amazingly talented Mike Porter.

My search for the right illustrator took over two years and I was beginning to wonder if I would ever find an artist with the style I was looking for. Then, thanks to a link on a writers' forum I belong to, I watched an animated poem on YouTube and knew that the person behind those illustrations was the perfect artist for my nursery rhymes. I felt incredibly fortunate when he agreed to take on the commission and from the earliest design sketches I knew that the 2-year wait had been worth it. My gratitude is boundless. Merci Mike!

Also thanks to the many poor followers of mine on social media who were the first audience for most of these poems during the inaugural Covid-19 lockdown in March 2020. Their willingness to laugh, comment and generally roll their eyes in a good natured way was what encouraged me to bring the poems out as a small collection.

Finally as always, to Jacki, for indulging my writing passions, being my best critic and my biggest supporter.

About the Author

Ian Hooper was born in Northern Ireland, served in the UK's Royal Air Force and now lives in the south west of Western Australia.

Writing under the pen name of Ian Andrew his first crime novel, Face Value, won the Publishers Weekly BookLife Prize for Fiction in 2017. Since then he has continued to add to that series of novels, is a successful short story writer, poet and ghost writer of both biographies and thrillers. He is also the director of Leschenault Press.

As Ian Andrew:

The Little Book of Silly Rhymes and Odd Verses

A Time To Every Purpose

Face Value

Flight Path

Fall Guys

Self-Publishing for Independent Authors